Tiger and Monkey

Written by Jill Eggleton
Illustrated by Philip Webb

Rigby

Tiger is asleep.
Monkey put a ribbon
on Tiger's tail.

2

3

Tiger woke up.
He looked at the ribbon.
He was **mad!**

5

Tiger went after Monkey.
But Monkey got away.

Monkey is asleep.
Tiger got Monkey's tail.
He tied it to a tree.

Monkey woke up.
He looked at his tail
and he was **mad!**

"Come here, Tiger!"
shouted Monkey.

"**No**," said Tiger.
"I am going to sleep."

A Sequence Chart

Guide Notes

Title: Tiger and Monkey
Stage: Early (2) – Yellow

Genre: Fiction
Approach: Guided Reading
Processes: Thinking Critically, Exploring Language, Processing Information
Written and Visual Focus: Sequence Chart, Speech Bubbles
Word Count: 83

THINKING CRITICALLY
(sample questions)
- What do you think this story could be about?
- Focus on the title and discuss.
- Why do you think Monkey put a ribbon around Tiger's tail?
- Why do you think Tiger was mad?
- What could Tiger have done instead of playing a trick on Monkey?
- What do you think Monkey might do next?

EXPLORING LANGUAGE

Terminology
Title, cover, illustrations, author, illustrator

Vocabulary
Interest words: ribbon, mad, tail, tied
High-frequency words: after, but, away, was, his
Positional words: on, up, out

Print Conventions
Capital letter for sentence beginnings and names (**T**iger, **M**onkey), periods,
quotation marks, commas, question mark, exclamation marks